TIME FLIES

DOWN TO THE LAST MINUTE

Written by Tara Lazar
Illustrated by Ross MacDonald

Little, Brown and Company
New York Boston

To the Punny Bunch—may we spend more time together soon!
—TL

For Milo and Chip
—RM

About This Book

The illustrations for this book were done in watercolor and colored pencil on Saunders watercolor paper, with wood letterpress printing type, and assembled in Photoshop. This book was edited by Mary-Kate Gaudet and designed by Lynn El-Roeiy and Véronique Lefèvre Sweet. The production was supervised by Lillian Sun, and the production editor was Marisa Finkelstein. The text was set in Sabon, and the display type is hand–lettered.

After dozing in my chair,
I had some time on my hands.

I grabbed my hat and decided to roam Capital City.
Ahh, crisp air, hubbub in the streets, and no problems…

But it wasn't long before trouble found me.
Yep, trouble with a capital T.

"Oh, Private I," said T, "I'm glad I ran into you."
I wasn't. He'd made me spill my latte.

"Do you have the time?" T asked.

"Time for what?" I replied. I got ready to spring into action.

"I mean, do you know what time it is? I must have lost my watch."

I glanced at my wrist. Strange—my watch was gone, too.
I could've sworn it was there a second ago.

I looked at the city clock. "The clock on City Jail has been stuck since yesterday," T said. "Both hands are up!"

Just then, **B** darted out of Café Uno.
"Come back here! Thief!"
she yelled after a mysterious figure.

T took off after the perp. I rushed over to B.
"What happened?" I asked.

"It was the oddest thing," said B.
"He yanked the clock off the wall
and just ran out."

I knew that time can get away,
but this was ridiculous.

I jotted down **B**'s
description of the
suspect and circled back
to my office.

There was no time to waste.

Uptown, I found the door ajar. T staggered in behind me. "Did you catch him?" I asked.

"No," T said, panting hard. "I need a time-out."

We sat down, and I noticed the clock on my desk was missing. This was alarming. And not alarming, now that my alarm wouldn't go off.

My phone started ringing and didn't stop all day.
Across the city, folks reported their timepieces disappearing.

Unfortunately, none of them had gotten a good look at the culprit.

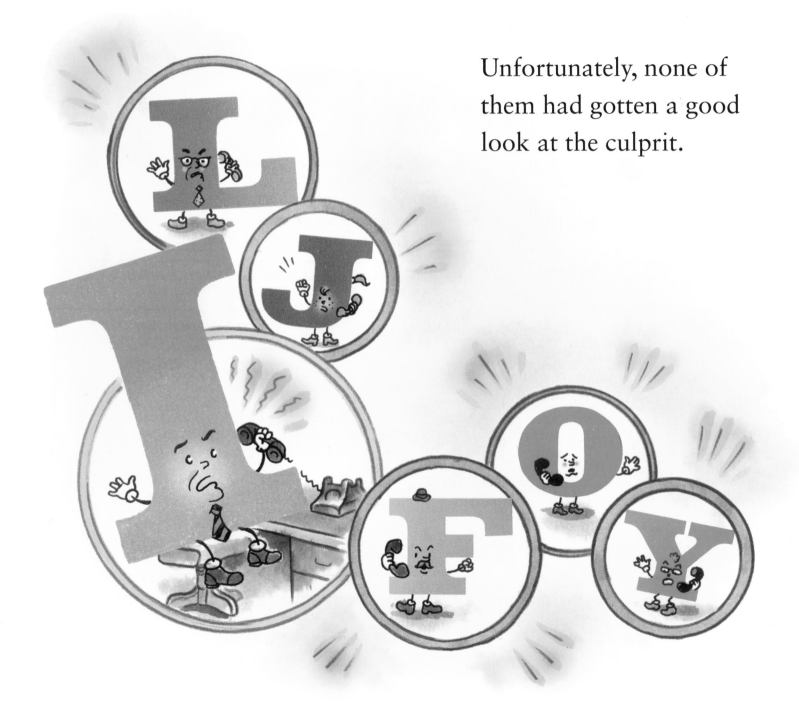

I interviewed Grandfather,
whose entire store was cleaned out.

This case was winding up
to be a full-time job.
I needed a solid lead.

I sat on my stoop to think.
I knew it was getting late when the sun
dipped low and shadows grew long.

The next morning, it dawned on me—there's one way to tell time that no one can ever take away.

I announced a citywide gathering at noon— at the sundial in Punctuation Park.

"You'll know it's noon when the sun's directly overhead," I said.

I staked out my position as a watchdog, and in no time, someone came along. Just as I'd suspected.

"Whatcha doing, Z?" I asked. "You're awfully early."
"Err, ahh—just setting up a tent for your gathering," Z said.

"But the tent would cast a shadow over the sundial...
and take away the last timepiece left in Capital City!"

As Z turned to run away, his pocket snagged on the sundial, and the truth was revealed.

"Z, you're the time bandit! You gave everyone a tough time!" Actually, he gave everyone no time at all.

"Okay, you got me!" exclaimed Z. "I don't want to be last anymore! I'm at the back of every line and the final name at roll call!"

So Z was at the end of his rope.

"I thought without clocks, everyone would be late. For once, I could be the first to show up," Z said.

"But you complete the alphabet, Z," I said.
"There wouldn't be an alphabet without you."

"Plus, being first isn't so peachy keen,"
said **A**, yawning. "I always have to
wake up early to kick things off. I'm
exhausted!"

"The middle can be uncomfortable, too," said L.

Aha, so that's why L's so skinny.

"And in the middle,
no one remembers who you are!
Everyone treats me like
a big zero!" said O.

"And don't forget," I said, "in every word game, Z scores the most points. You're worth so much more than you think!"

And with that, Z apologized for causing a whole lotta disorder. No time like the present.

But the Grammar Police got the last word. "Come along, Z. You'll have to serve hard time."

And so I had cracked another case, which was no surprise.

I'm known for catching Z's.